LEGALLY
CORRECT
FAIRY TALES

LEGALLY
CORRECT
FAIRY TALES

DAVID FISHER

WARNER BOOKS

A Time Warner Company

Copyright © 1996 by David Fisher
All rights reserved.

Warner Books, Inc., 1271 Avenue of the Americas, New York, NY 10020

 A Time Warner Company

Printed in the United States of America
First Printing: September 1996
10   9   8   7   6   5   4

Library of Congress Cataloging-in-Publication Data

Fisher, David
    Legally correct fairy tales / David Fisher.
        p. cm.
    ISBN 0-446-52075-6
    1. Law—Humor. 2. Fairy tales—Humor. I. Title.
PN6231.L4F57 1996
813'.54—dc20   96-3491
                                                  CIP

Book design, illustrations, and composition by Giorgetta Bell McRee

To my mother, Sylvia Fisher,
a mother, mother-in-law, and grandmother
of lawyers. Enough is enough.

ACKNOWLEDGMENTS

There are many people I would like to mention here; however, the lawyers have informed me I am limited by current libel laws. That stated, I would like to thank my editor, Rick Wolff, who goes to bat for authors whenever a hit is needed; as well as my agent for this project, Frank Weimann, for another job well done. I would also like to thank Susan Koenig for her valuable guidance and unfailing support.

Contents

LEGALLY CORRECT FAIRY TALES

JACK "DOE" AND JILL "DOE" V. IMPERIAL BUCKET CORPORATION

he Plaintiffs, Jack "Doe" and Jill "Doe," both minors, do hereby allege that (1) they suffered grievous and permanent injuries when a steel bucket manufactured by the Defendant, Imperial Bucket Corporation, proved to be of unsafe design and manufacture, and without proper safety guards, so as to allow it to be operated in an unsafe manner by these minors; and (2) the Defendant is guilty of such gross product liability as to be responsible for these injuries and therefore should compensate Jack and Jill for a sum greater than five million dollars ($5,000,000).

Plaintiffs were both completely untrained in the proper operation of the Defendant's bucket, hereinafter referred to as "the pail," when they attempted to convey such pail up a steep incline, hereinafter referred to as "the hill."

The pail manufactured by the Defendant was made of steel and weighed 1.6 pounds when empty. It was designed to be carried by a rounded metal handle, or "bail." Depending on the material used to fill the pail, the weight of such pail could vary between 1.9 pounds (cotton) and 61.0 pounds (pig iron). Unless one received proper instruction in the use of this pail, it could easily be overloaded, causing it to become unstable.

The pail included no directions for safe use, no warnings of any kind about the potential danger of the pail, and no safety devices to protect individuals from suffering injuries when using this pail. The pail could be operated by minors who could not possibly be aware of the inherent dangers in the defective design of this pail and would therefore be subject to injury.

Jack and Jill will testify that they were able to move forward in a skipping (def.: proceed with leaps and bounds) manner up the hill, holding on to the pail, which swung precariously between them. Upon reaching the top of said hill, they proceeded to fill the pail with a clear liquid, hereinafter referred to as "water." The weight of the water will be affixed through laboratory testing. What they could not possibly have known is that the defective design of this pail permitted it to be filled with water to an unsafe level.

As Plaintiffs began carrying the now hazardous steel pail down the side of said hill, the water began shifting in the pail, causing the weight to be unevenly distributed. While this motion, known scientifically as "sloshing," did cause a partial reduction in the contents of the pail, this had the effect of causing an additional unbalancing of the pail. Jack and Jill, neither being experienced in the trade of carrying a pail of water down a steep incline, suffered extreme difficulty in maintaining control over the pail. In their effort to retain control of the pail, both Jack and Jill, individually and simultaneously, did lose their balance owing entirely to the instability of the pail.

According to police reports, Jack apparently lost control of the pail and fell down the hill. Jill, a young female weighing approximately forty-eight pounds, could not possibly have been expected to retain control of the pail without assistance and immediately came tumbling after.

By reason of the foregoing and by reason of the Defendant's negligence, Plaintiffs were severely bruised, injured, and wounded; suffered, and still suffer, and will continue to suffer for some time to come, physical and mental pain and great bodily injuries. Specifically, Jack broke his crown in three different places in addition to fracturing his ribs and right arm. Jill sustained bruises and contusions to her legs, ankles, and wrist. Some of these injuries may well be of a permanent nature so as to affect the lives of these minors forever and one day.

The Imperial Bucket Corporation, being aware for an indeterminate time that the bucket they callously manufactured and offered to market had serious design flaws and under certain conditions could cause severe injury, nevertheless did continue to manufacture and market such a bucket to the public. They failed to take the necessary steps to inform the public of the potential for injury inherent in the use of their product. That they did so, and continue to do so, indicates a disregard for the public welfare, for which punitive damages might be deemed appropriate.

Until such design problems as noted are corrected, the Imperial Bucket Corporation should be enjoined from offering their product for sale to the public. They should also be required to recall all such defective buckets in existence and make appropriate restitution and repairs. All persons past and present in possession of this dangerous product should receive notice that under certain conditions, *even with proper precautions,* use of this product might result in permanent, disabling injury. Minors should be prevented from purchasing or possessing this product without proper parental supervision.

Due to use of this defective product, Jack "Doe" and Jill "Doe," minors, have suffered irreparable injury and must be compensated in line with the substantial pain and suffering they have endured.

Tailor v. Emperor
Motion for Summary Judgment

n this action, the Plaintiff, Donald Tailor, by trade a tailor of fine garments, hereby alleges and swears that he was employed by agents of the Emperor to create for the Emperor a suit of new clothes. This suit of clothes was to be worn by the Emperor when he led the annual parade down Emperor's

Way on Emperor's Day. Tailor Tailor asserts that he was told to use only the finest materials, cut to measurements provided by Palace officials, and to create a design traditional yet au courant. Plaintiff Tailor asserts that on at least three previous occasions he was employed to design, cut, and sew garments for the Emperor and on each such prior occasion he was suitably compensated by the Emperor. Plaintiff Tailor asserts he is a highly respected craftsman whose garments have been worn by royalty in kingdoms, fiefdoms, dukedoms, counties, and towns throughout the Empire.

Plaintiff Tailor asserts that three days prior to the parade he did deliver to the Palace a newly constructed suit of garments, including underclothing, knee socks, knickers, a formal shirt with high collar, and a long tea coat. These clothes are described by the Plaintiff as "avant-garde" and "a fashion statement beyond description." After a fitting, the Emperor accepted these garments. The Emperor then agreed to pay Plaintiff Tailor the agreed-upon fee plus a bonus. The garments were unique, constructed from a new material, described by Plaintiff Tailor as "a miracle fabric. This is the most sheer material ever produced, woven from a combination of unicorn fur and pig hair. This material has been found to be amazingly light in weight, incredibly smooth to the touch, and spectacularly beautiful to the eye [see attached Exhibits 1 and 1A]. This material will never wrinkle. It will not stain, tear, or show wear of any kind no matter how much abuse it sustains. It can be folded many times to fit into the smallest luggage. It is extremely simple to accessorize. It will even change size to compensate for changes in the wearer. Upon viewing this suit for the first time, the Emperor commented, 'I've never seen anything like it before.'"

Unfortunately, during the parade an uneducated child with an untrained eye unable to appreciate the subtleties of this garment did remark that he could not see the true beauty, causing the Emperor to believe that something was amiss with this suit. Notwithstanding that the rank and file in the Palace did praise and compliment the clothing, the Emperor accepted the word of a minor and has refused to pay the agreed-upon fee. Plaintiff Tailor asks for immediate payment for the garments.

Plaintiff also asserts that, contrary to the uneducated opinion voiced by a child, royalty in this and other kingdoms have ordered garments made from the same "miracle fabric" as that of the Emperor. Plaintiff Tailor has received so many orders that his shop is currently backlogged and he cannot produce them rapidly enough, as production of this material is painstaking and time-consuming. Plaintiff Tailor charges that his reputation has been damaged and he has been subjected to derision. He humbly requests that the Court order the Emperor to make immediate payment for services faithfully rendered.

FOR THE DEFENSE: In this action, the Defendant, our Most Honored and Beloved Emperor, Direct Descendant of the Sun King and Moon Queen, does hereby assert that he employed the Plaintiff to create for him a suit of clothing suitable for wearing in the annual Emperor's Day Parade. However, the Emperor asserts that when such garments were delivered to him, the suit in question was the wrong color and the wrong size and appeared to have been previously worn. Plaintiff did additional work on these garments and did deliver to the Palace the morning of the parade several hangers on which he claimed garments constructed from this "miracle fabric" were hanging. When the Emperor did not fully appreciate the beauty of this fabric, Plaintiff explained it was so unusually sheer that it looked like nothing but in fact was special, unique, one of a kind. The Emperor did accept this clothing and did wear this clothing in the parade. He was subjected to scorn, ridicule, embarrassment, and humiliation. The Emperor does not like to be subjected to scorn, ridicule, embarrassment, and humiliation. Therefore he refused payment to the Plaintiff based on the fact that Plaintiff failed to deliver to him suitable clothing at the proper time. The Emperor humbly asks the Court to dismiss all claims against him.

DECISION OF JUDGE LAW: I see absolutely nothing to dispute here. The Emperor did not receive satisfaction or clothing. Therefore he should not be forced to pay for it. Plaintiff's motion for summary judgment is DENIED.

EXHIBITS 1 AND 1A: The suit made of "miracle fabric," front (*left*) and back (*right*) views.

KINGDOM V. HANSEL AND GRETEL

Report to the Court: Defendants' State of Mind at the Time of Fatal Accident; Submitted to the Court, Dr. Kiddlove, M.A., B.A., B.S., Department of Child Psychology, University of the Kingdom at Magic Hallow

Dr. I. M. Kiddlove, did examine extensively the minor Defendants, Hansel and Gretel, over a prolonged period of time. I conducted extensive interviews with the Defendants on at least five occasions, both individually and together, and have spent approximately twenty hours with them. I

believe this statement to be a true reflection of their psychological state at the time of the alleged incident.

FACTS AT ISSUE: The Defendants, Hansel and Gretel, minor brother and sister, are known to be the only children of a poor woodsman. It is alleged by the Defendants that their father did intentionally and knowingly abandon and desert them in the dark forest to please a stepmother. It is alleged by these minor Defendants that they wandered aimlessly through this forest until, starving, they encountered the ranch-style house at Number One Wilderness Lane, such house being made completely of gingerbread and mortified sugar icing. At such time, starving, they began to eat the first floor of this home, seriously weakening the structure. There is a belief upon statements that Hansel and Gretel were psychologically abused by a father suffering from pronounced *macho deficita,* who acceded to the demands of a strong female presence.

The Defendants were halted in their destruction of the property by the legal owner, Mrs. Josefa Crone. According to the Defendants, Ms. Crone, an elderly woman of indeterminate age, claimed to be a witch. Both Hansel and Gretel state that they were afraid of this individual and her potential power to harm them. Defendants state that the owner of the property locked Hansel in a cage and threatened to eat him when he was sufficiently fattened. Defendants state that Ms. Crone suffered from *cannaseefaraway* (farsightedness) and would go near this cage daily to determine if Hansel had gained weight. Defendants state that to save Hansel, they showed Ms. Crone a chicken bone, which she mistakenly accepted as Hansel's finger. After a considerable period of time, during which Defendants acknowledge they were adequately fed, clothed, and provided shelter, Ms. Crone announced her intention to cook and eat Hansel. This statement was not perceived by either Defendant as attempted humor. After turning on the oven and preheating it to a temperature of approximately 350 degrees Fahrenheit, she leaned closer to determine if it was hot enough to cook a boy, at which point Gretel, in conspiracy with Hansel, pushed Ms. Crone into the oven, broiling her. Defendants state they subsequently consumed one room of the house to gain strength, then fled to freedom. Defendants state that at all times they acted in self-defense.

DAVID FISHER

REPORT OF DR. KIDDLOVE

Courts in this kingdom have long labored to answer the question "Who is crazy?" Many crazy people have appeared in the courtrooms of this kingdom. Yet the question remains, can we morally convict crazy people who are guilty of a crime? Or, conversely, are we crazy not to convict guilty people of criminal actions? Is it crazy to find a guilty person not guilty because that person is crazy?

Here we have two young adults who state they believed at all times that their lives were endangered and therefore took the actions they deemed necessary to save their lives. In many such cases (*Kingdom* v. *Menendez*, cit. 34 part B, 1994) the courts have found that individuals acting in what they believed to be self-defense are protected by the same laws as if they actually were in jeopardy and cannot be judged guilty of the results of those actions. The question in this matter is, did Hansel and Gretel believe in their hearty-heart-heart that in fact their lives were in danger? Did they act in self-defense?

It is of no consequence, nor is it possible, to determine at this point in time if the deceased, Ms. Crone, was legally a witch. Being bad, harboring

16

negative thoughts, making threats, even casting spells under certain conditions, does not fulfill the legal definition of witch. If she was not a witch, but Hansel and Gretel believed she was a witch, they were suffering from advanced paranoia, and the actions they took grew out of that paranoia. Therefore the Defendants were of diminished mind and cannot be found guilty of this crime. If, however, the deceased actually was a witch, Hansel and Gretel took reasonable actions to protect their lives and cannot be found guilty of this crime.

On the surface the facts may make it difficult to accept the possibility that these two children were in danger. To many, it may appear that they ran away from home because they did not receive the love and attention to which they were entitled as children and came upon the home of a hermit living alone in the woods. This very old woman immediately claimed to be a witch. While some people may suspect that a very old woman, living by herself in the woods and claiming to have magical powers, might be suffering from dementia, i.e., "nutty as a fruitcake" (Robbins, *Old Women Claiming to Be Witches*, Macmillan, 1945), the question at all times is not what is real, but what did the Defendants *believe* to be real at the time of the incident, resulting in the untimely broiling of the deceased.

It has been seen throughout the legal history of this kingdom that facts are subject to the interpretation of lawyers. Facts, in fact, may not be factual, unless they are proven beyond a shadow of a doubt. Conversely, something proven beyond a shadow of a doubt may be presumed to be a fact, even though it is provably untrue. It is for that reason defendants are adjudged "not guilty" rather than innocent. Innocent people can be guilty, while people not guilty may not be innocent.

Research has proven that children believe what children believe. And what children believe may not square directly with the facts as they occur, but rather with the facts as they are perceived. This means that children not directly in danger may believe that they are in danger, and therefore they are in danger and may take actions to save their lives, even though their lives are not in jeopardy.

Whether or not this woman was a witch is not significant. When asked in several interviews if they thought she was a witch, Hansel and Gretel responded in the affirmative. There is much proof to support this contention. The Defendants claim that Hansel was locked in a cage and Gretel was forced to cook and clean. Although this was an aged woman, perhaps weak and infirm and certainly unable to protect herself against two healthy young adults, the fact that they believed she was a witch and was capable of casting spells against them is sufficient reason to understand their compliance to her demands. And whether the cage in which Hansel was locked was real or metaphorical is not significant. We, as human beings, often find ourselves locked in metaphorical cages, which are just as real as cages with iron bars and secure locks. Therefore Hansel, because he believed he was locked in a cage, was in fact locked in a cage, whether he was locked in a cage or not.

As to the instigation of the action taken against Ms. Crone, threats made or imagined may be real if they are perceived to be threats. Threats do not need to be spoken or even suggested by actions or manner to be perceived as threats. As the noted Dr. Schlocker wrote in his well-received thesis, *The Eternal Triangle: Me, Myself, and I,* "We are precisely what we believe we are (with the exception of height). If we believe we are inferior, we take inferior actions. If we believe we are unattractive, we take unattractive actions. It is when we believe we are what we want to be, that we are." In this case that is precisely what is at issue: Did Hansel and Gretel believe that they were prisoners and that their collective lives were endangered by an adult capable of exercising power against them?

The psyche is an unusual and oft dangerous part of the mind. It is believed by many scholars to be the seat of psychosis. Consistent throughout all my interviews with Hansel and Gretel was their belief that they were in danger. There can be no argument with the fact that they had come from a broken home: their father had taken them into the woods and abandoned them, their natural mother had disappeared, and their stepmother did not want them. These elements often create a disturbance in a youthful mind. And such is arguably the case here. Were Hansel and Gretel psychotic? Did they imagine an old lady was a witch? Is it possible a form of mass hysteria led them to believe that she was going to cook and eat Hansel? Were their actions irrational but based on rational thought?

The answers to these questions must be a very firm yes and no. The field of psychiatry is not paved with artificial turf. There are few true bounces on this field, and the path of an object is not predictable: anything can happen. But if it is crazy to kill another human being, every person who kills must be crazy and therefore cannot be convicted of murder because they are protected by law. Hansel and Gretel readily confessed to killing Ms. Crone, who may or may not have been a witch. They admit this act. Since killing an individual is a crime that may be penalized by imprisonment or death, anyone who confesses to a murder must be considered crazy, since it would be crazy to confess to an act that would lead directly to a deprivation of life or liberty.

Knowing this, we must acknowledge that since Hansel and Gretel confessed to this act, they cannot be convicted. If, however, they claimed they did not commit this act, they would be perfectly sane and could be considered guilty of the crime.

That is my finding in this case.

Petition for Guardianship
and Other Legal Relief
in the Matter of
Beauty, Sleeping

he petitioner, Mr. King, hereby requests (1) that an order be issued by this Court prohibiting any or all extraordinary or heroic measures being taken now or at any time in the future to resuscitate, awaken, or in any way revive or sustain by artificial means their relation by blood, Sleeping Beauty; and that

no experimental treatment be administered and no persons unknown to this Court through its trustees be permitted access to said Beauty.

(2) that the petitioner, Mr. King, and his spouse be named now and forever after legal guardians of the subject, trustees of all assets, and, in the event of her death, executors of her estate.

THE FACTS: The aforementioned Beauty has been surviving for seventy-one years in a trance-like state consistent in every way with the medical condition coma. This state was induced by an unknown drug injected into her system with a needle. The unknown chemical substance, injected either knowingly or unwittingly on or about the subject's sixteenth birthday, did cause grievous damage to her central nervous system and brain stem. This hallucinogenic substance did also cause similar harm to others engaged in the service of Beauty and believed to have had marginal physical contact with the subject. The immediate result of such drug introduction was a total and complete loss of consciousness, the inability to communicate in any form whatsoever with any persons, and the complete and total cessation of all bodily functions save breathing.

There is no proven antidote to this drug. The

source, or sorcerer, of this drug is unknown to the petitioner.

Beauty, Sleeping, remains in such a trancelike state as described to this date. She has not responded to any attempt to revive her with traditional, proven, safe, and accepted means of resuscitation.

The petitioner claims knowledge that a person or persons not specifically known to said petitioner have made or will make heroic attempts to revive Beauty, Sleeping, using a highly experimental treatment medically referred to as "artificial respiration" (def.: breathing through unnatural means), commonly known as "mouth-to-mouth resuscitation." There is no evidence of any kind to support the use of said treatment in this case. Additionally, as the drug known to have caused the subject's condition has officially been labeled a "dangerous drug," whose properties have not sufficiently been tested, and which drug is proved to have caused the onset of similar symptoms to persons having only casual contact with Beauty, there exists a clear and present danger to the general populace that any type of physical contact with the subject may result in uncontrolled spread of such symptoms.

Petitioner thereby, to protect the general well-being, requests a court order be issued immediately prohibiting such experimental treatment by any and all persons whosoever now or at any time in the forever after.

The petitioner also requests the Court decree that should the physical state of the subject change in any way, shape, or form, no measures except those currently accepted by the medical community as immediate aid to lessen pain and suffering be employed in her behalf. It is the wish of the petitioners that no artificial or mechanical means of any kind known now or at any time in the future be used in this case to extend the condition in which Beauty currently resides.

At the commencement of this drug-induced trance, Beauty, Sleeping, was in possession of a substantial amount of material goods, including but not limited to items of pure gold, jewelry, acreage, and a castle (one). Such holdings were put into a trust to be administered by her blood relatives at the commencement of this current state. Those people charged with supervising said trust have perished through primarily (but not limited to) natural causes, such as age and war. In the absence of supervision, the value of such holdings has substantially increased, but without proper legal authority to oversee such holdings, there exists significant risk of loss or depreciation of the value of such holdings. The petitioner hereby declares to the Court that any and all members of the immediate family of the subject, Beauty (including but not limited to father, mother, siblings of any gender, cousins by blood first through sixth, aunts, and uncles), have perished and the petitioner is the sole surviving blood relation. The petitioner voluntarily relinquishes all rights to privacy for matters relating to this claim and will make available to this Court samples necessary for the scientific establishment of this blood link through any and all known means.

As the sole surviving blood relation of Beauty, Sleeping, the petitioner requests that the Court appoint him legal guardian of Beauty, Sleeping, with full power of attorney and such access to herein described trust to enable full and proper management of these assets to the benefit of Beauty, Sleeping, her heirs, and her estate in total.

In the event of the untimely death of Beauty, Sleeping, the petitioner humbly requests that the Court appoint the petitioner sole executor of the estate of the subject, with full powers to take such actions as necessary to benefit the estate of Beauty, Sleeping, now or at any time forever and ever.

Re Snow White, Inc.

Notice to Cure under Penalty of Law

his is an official complaint issued by the Equal Employment Opportunity Commission (EEOC) of this kingdom to inform and notify <u>Snow White, Inc.,</u> that you are in violation of kingdom laws prohibiting discrimination, that you have failed to comply with prevailing equal employment statutes, that you must cease and desist such policies that have resulted in the issuance of this citation and take immediately steps to cure any and all listed violations.

WHEREAS and wherefore the government of the people of this kingdom have decreed, under Article XV, Section 3.4, subparagraph 8a, of the Uniform Code of Kingdom Labor Practices, that no one shall be deprived of the right of employment based on gender, age, color, race, religion, education, physical capability, intelligence, magical abilities, or any other unique or distinguishing characteristic, it is hereby alleged that <u>Snow White, Inc.,</u> doing business as <u>Snow White and the Seven Dwarfs,</u> a mining, maintenance, and food preparation concern, did knowingly violate the above-identified Kingdom Labor Laws by employing individuals known collectively as "The Seven Dwarfs" and individually as Doc, Grumpy, Sneezy, Bashful, Happy, Sleepy, and Dopey, to the exclusion of all other applicants able to perform such tasks as appropriate under the Uniform Employment Contract.

As defined in the Uniform Code of Kingdom Labor Practices, as issued by the Equal Employment Opportunity Commission, maintenance and food preparation are non-licensed industries, subject to periodic inspection by Kingdom Health Boards, and as such require minimum training (see *Kingdom* v. *Hooters*). Employees are required to advertise such employment opportunities in a minimum of three different locales or publications.

It is alleged that <u>Snow White, Inc.,</u> did fail to advertise such positions as were available. It is further alleged that <u>Snow White, Inc.,</u> hired for these positions seven individuals, all of them male, all of them Caucasian, all of them under four feet (48 inches) in height. Such an employment pattern has been determined by kingdom courts to be "discrimination prima facie," discrimination in your face, and is in violation of prior court rulings and must be cured within the proscribed period of time.

<u>Snow White, Inc.,</u> must submit to this agency within forty-five (45) business days a plan to cure this violation by hiring nonmale, non-Caucasian, nonshort people. This plan must include provisions for employing a minimum of one-third of the hiring of the workforce in a nondiscriminatory fashion. This may be done by increasing the size of the workforce or replacing current workers with people eligible for employment under this act. If an

acceptable plan is not submitted to this agency within forty-five (45) business days of issuance of this notice, this agency may take steps, including imposition of penalties, to prevent <u>Snow White, Inc.,</u> from continuing to operate in a discriminatory manner. Such penalties may include fines and the loss of all licenses under which they are currently operating; it may also include the right to cause a cessation of operations as long as the company remains in violation of EEOC regulations.

USA v. Wolf

Deposition of Mr. Wolf
For the Court: Richard Langsam,
United States Attorney's Office,
Southern District

hese being the true words of: Thaddeus Wolf, who voluntarily appeared before this hearing on the <u>15th</u> day of <u>October,</u> of the year noted below:

COURT: For the record, the government of the United States of America has brought charges of corruption, fraud, and illegal control of

DAVID FISHER

specific building trades unions to be enumerated, against both named and unnamed individuals known collectively as "the Wolf Family," under the federal statute known as the Racketeering Influenced Corrupt Organization (RICO) Act. Under this statute it is a criminal act to participate in or have knowledge of two or more crimes and/or act as a member of a group constituted to perform illegal acts. Mr. Wolf is believed to be an active member of the Wolf Family.

COURT: Thank you for coming today, Mr. Wolf.

MR. WOLF: Yeah, sure. I mean, what else was I gonna do, lie around the woods all day? I'd rather lie around here. (LAUGHTER) That's a joke, see.

COURT: I see. Now, Mr. Wolf, is it not true you are known among your associates by the nickname "Big Bad"?

MR. WOLF: They call me a lot of things, but I never heard that one. Hey, you know, people call you a lot of things behind your tail. Maybe you're referring to the fact that my wife calls me "Big Dad."

COURT: Mr. Wolf, are you a member of an organized crime family known collectively as "the Wolf Family"?

MR. WOLF: That's your joke, right?

COURT: I assure you, Mr. Wolf, the Court does not mean to be amusing.

MR. WOLF: Oh, okay. Sorry. But let me tell you, my family, the Wolfs, the last thing I would call them is organized. I mean, on a Saturday morning when I'm ready to go hunting, it takes everybody else hours to get ready. These people wouldn't be able to find their lair without a road map. Organized? Nah, that's just something you read in the papers.

COURT: Mr. Wolf, are you familiar with an individual known as Little Red Riding Hood?

MR. WOLF: Red Riding Hook? Nah, I don't think so.

COURT: That's Hood, Mr. Wolf, Red Riding Hood.

MR. WOLF: Red Riding Hood? Red Riding Hood? No, I don't think I know of the gentleman. Is he any relation to Robin Hood?

COURT: How about Peter? I suppose you've never heard of him?

MR. WOLF: Peter, huh? I don't know nothin' about any Peter having to do with a Wolf.

COURT: To your knowledge, have you or any member of the Wolf Family ever dressed in sheep's clothing?

MR. WOLF: Oh, now come on, I object to that. I come here on my own, trying to help out you guys, and you're gonna sit there and call me names? What is that? What do you think I am? You think I'm gonna just sit here and let people think I would go around dressed as some kind of friggin' sheep?

COURT: Please answer the question, Mr. Wolf. Did you or any member of the Wolf Family dress in sheep's clothing?

MR. WOLF: No. Okay? Happy now?

COURT: Mr. Wolf, do you know the Little-Pigg brothers?

MR. WOLF: Let me think. The British guys, right? There's three of them. They're building contractors, I think. Yeah, maybe I met 'em once or twice.

COURT: Would you describe your relationship with them?

MR. WOLF: We didn't have no real relationship. I met 'em maybe a few times at most.

COURT: Are you now or have you ever been an officer of the Construction and Building Materials Union Local 145?

MR. WOLF: Yeah, sure. I got my card probably about twelve years ago.

COURT: And precisely what is your position in that union?

MR. WOLF: Vice president. I sell building materials. You know, all kinds.

COURT: Have you ever sold building materials to the Little-Pigg Construction Company?

MR. WOLF: I sell to a lot of people. If they build, I probably sold them materials.

COURT: Mr. Wolf, did you ever threaten the Little-Piggs with violence if they did not purchase materials from you?

MR. WOLF: Me? Threaten somebody? Listen to this guy. Where do you get your jokes, the Grimm Brothers? (LAUGHTER)

COURT: In fact, did you not warn them that

unless they purchased all their construction materials from you at highly inflated prices, you would blow up their houses?

MR. WOLF: That's ridiculous. The only things I ever blow up are those plastic rafts for my kids to float on in the pool.

COURT: Oh, I'm sorry, I've misread this document. Let me quote Mr. Little-Pigg's previous testimony before this Court: "He told me that if I didn't buy steel from him, he and his boys were going to blow DOWN my house." Now, Mr. Wolf, do you recall that conversation?

MR. WOLF: What do you expect from a guy like that? The guy's a Little-Pigg.

COURT: Mr. Wolf, please. Just answer the question.

MR. WOLF: You sure you're not confusing the Wolfs with the Fox Family? I could tell you stories about the Foxes that'd—

COURT: Mr. Wolf, just answer the question.

MR. WOLF: Nah, it's all made up. It's just a fantasy.

COURT: And, in fact, when the Little-Pigg brothers did build a residence primarily out of hay purchased from a nonunion supplier, did you and your hired henchpeople not appear outside that house and threaten to destroy it?

MR. WOLF: This is like a fairy tale. I never heard such lies since that little kid cried he'd seen me outside his house.

COURT: I would like to enter as People's Exhibit One the following recording. It is an audiotape. On it can be heard the voices of the Little-Piggs calling 911 and requesting immediate assistance. (RECORDER SET UP)

OPERATOR'S VOICE: Nine one one.

LITTLE-PIGG: Help! Help! You gotta come quick. There's a wolf outside and he's trying to blow down my house. He's really in a huff!

You've heard that, Mr. Wolf. Does that refresh your memory?

MR. WOLF: You kidding? He can't even act scared. That ham.

COURT: Mr. Wolf, the record shows that, in fact,

that home was subsequently destroyed in a high wind.

MR. WOLF: What does that have to do with me? I told him if he used inferior materials, that house would never stand up. If he bought from me, I'll bet you that house would be standing today.

COURT: When the first Little-Pigg brother managed to escape into the home of the second Little-Pigg, a house constructed primarily of wood beams and siding purchased from a nonunion source, did not you and/or your henchpeople once again appear outside that house and threaten to blow it down? Specifically, and I quote, "To huff and puff and to blow your house down"?

MR. WOLF: Have those Little-Piggs been smoking something?

COURT: Are you refusing to answer the question?

MR. WOLF: You know, this is exactly how rumors get going. I went over to their house, okay? To welcome them to the neighborhood. Personally, I figured it was a nice thing to do. This is a pretty nice neighborhood, and they built these little shacks. You know what it does to real estate values when Little-Piggs move in? But no, I was gonna be

Mr. Nice Guy. So I go over there and they wouldn't even open the door. My wife had baked a cake for them, you know, it was sort of like . . . Welcome Wagon.

COURT: So you didn't threaten to eat them?

MR. WOLF: Eat them? I invited them for dinner. But it's possible they misunderstood.

COURT: And you did not threaten that if they squealed to the police, you would have them for breakfast?

MR. WOLF: Do I have to listen to this stuff? They don't speak so good.

COURT: And when they retreated to the second Little-Pigg's house, did you not again threaten them with personal harm? Please listen to People's Exhibit Two:

> UNIDENTIFIED VOICE: Come out, come out, or I'll blow your house down.

Now, Mr. Wolf, does that voice sound familiar?

MR. WOLF: Robin Williams? I love the guy.

COURT: That wasn't you?

41

MR. WOLF: Me? You kidding or what? I wasn't near that place that day, whenever it was. And I can prove it. It was probably kids. You know how they like to cause trouble for strangers.

COURT: Let the record show that that house was subsequently destroyed by strong winds.

MR. WOLF: Don't blame me for that. If they'd have bought their materials from me like I suggested, that house would still be standing. But when you buy cheap stuff, that's what happens.

COURT: Now, let us move to the third Little-Pigg home, this one constructed of brick and mortar.

MR. WOLF: So they got smart and finally built a good solid house.

COURT: Did you not threaten to blow down that house, too?

MR. WOLF: See, see, that's what I mean. I never threatened nobody. I wanted to give them a demonstration of the value of using quality material. I showed them how it could withstand strong winds.

COURT: I would now like to enter People's Exhibit Three:

> UNIDENTIFIED VOICE: . . . huff and puff and blow your house down. (STRONG WINDS)

Now, Mr. Wolf, is that not you?

MR. WOLF: Yeah, maybe it's me, but this is taken completely out of context.

COURT: Sir, is it your testimony that that is not you attempting to blow down this house?

MR. WOLF: Lemme finish, okay? I have very bad asthma. I mean, you listen to my doctor, I've got two paws in the grave. He's always after me to move to Arizona or someplace dry. I see what you mean about this sounding like me, but it's not. That's me just trying to breathe.

COURT: Mr. Wolf, do you have anything else you'd like to say to this court?

MR. WOLF: Just that I don't know where you people get these stories from. Those Little-Piggs are a sty on the whole neighborhood, and they're just trying to blame their problems on self-respecting individuals such as myself. And that's all I have to say.

COURT: Thank you for coming today.

MR. WOLF: And I didn't wear no little sheep's clothes, either.

Transcribed and attested to:

Teri Public
_____

[N. O. Teri Public]

Humpty Dumpty v. King, King's Hospital, All of King's Horses, All of King's Men

HUMPTY DUMPTY
Plaintiff

against

KING'S HOSPITAL
Defendant

laintiffs as and for their Verified Complaint, allege the following, upon information and belief:

CAUSE OF ACTION
(1) At all times hereinafter mentioned Defendant facility was and still is a corporation wholly owned and operated by the King, the royal family, and heirs,

under the existing laws of this kingdom, as established by the King, to be a profit-making entity.

(2) At all times the Defendant facility did operate with permission from the King, and was duly empowered to perform any and all medical services deemed appropriate, and did operate under a medical license issued by the King that permitted them to practice internal medicine, external medicine, invasive surgery, reconstructive surgery, and basic and advanced sorcery.

(3) Defendants, their respective agents, servants, and/or employees were negligent in the medical treatment rendered to and on behalf of Plaintiff, HUMPHREY DUMPTY, were careless, departed from accepted medical practice, performed contraindicated procedures, failed to perform indicated procedures, and in other respects failed to follow good and accepted medical practice and therefore have committed malpractice against the Plaintiff.

(4) As a result of the foregoing, Plaintiff was permanently injured, permanently deformed, suffers pain and anguish and embarrassment, incurred expenses and lost earnings, and was permanently disabled.

(5) Defendants failed to advise Plaintiff of the risks, hazards, and dangers inherent in the treat-

ment and surgery, failed to advise of the alternatives thereto, and failed to obtain and inform consent.

(6) As a result of the foregoing, Plaintiff was permanently damaged to a sum in excess of two million dollars ($2,000,000) in real damages and four million dollars ($4,000,000) in punitive damages.

THE FACTS

(1) On the fourth day of June in this year of the King, Mr. Humphrey "Humpty" Dumpty was walking on Kings Lane, in Kingstown, when a sudden and severe rain shower caused him to take shelter beneath several large trees. Mr. Dumpty did thereupon endeavor to await the conclusion of said shower by sitting on a high stone wall. There were no warning signs of any kind in proximity to this wall. There were no barriers of any kind, including but not limited to fences, gates, or concertina wire, preventing access to this wall. There were no guards of any kind, including but not limited to human guards and guard dogs, preventing access to this wall. Therefore Mr. Dumpty did unknowingly climb upon a dangerous and unprotected wall and must not be seen to be liable for his subsequent injury.

(2) The uppermost surface of this wall, the north side, had become covered with a substance consistent in every way with "moss." When exposed to moisture, moss will become extremely slippery, a natural defect in this product.

(3) The wall was approximately six (6) feet high, constructed of stone and rock held together with mortar. Architect and contractor of the wall is presently unknown. Mr. Dumpty did take refuge upon this wall. After several minutes a strong gust of wind did exacerbate prior existing unsafe conditions, causing Mr. Dumpty to fall off this wall through no individual cause and effect. Mr. Dumpty did fall a great distance and did suffer serious and severe injuries upon making physical contact with the ground.

(4) Such great fall did have the immediate consequences of causing Mr. Dumpty to fail to enjoy a state of consciousness for a prolonged period of time. Plaintiff did resume a state of consciousness in King's Hospital, awakening to find himself totally and completely unrecognizable, in a state of disrepair, cracked and glued, misshapen, disfigured, unovaled, and otherwise transformed, causing severe pain and anguish, mental duress, and prolonged shock.

(5) Prior to this accident, Plaintiff was in good

health, good mind, and good repair. He suffered no permanent disabling impediments. Subsequent to treatment in King's Hospital, Plaintiff suffered from and continues to suffer from pain, anguish, and disfigurement; he has become the object of scorn and ridicule; he has become a recluse and cannot leave his home; he has lost the love and affection of family and friends; he has been unable to work. Mr. Dumpty has become a shell of his former self.

(6) The foregoing is due to the negligence of the King's men. Document A140-3, a standard hospital admittance form, describes Mr. Dumpty's injuries as "shattered outer shell resulting in numerous and severe splintering into small and jagged pieces. Loss of said protective shell caused severe hemorrhaging of internal matter, resulting in 'scrambling' of patient's mind. Patient was in critical condition when received at King's Hospital. Patient's cholesterol level was 100 percent, indicating severe trauma and dictating use of emergency lifesaving techniques."

(7) At King's Hospital the King's doctors attempted to fix and repair Plaintiff's wounds and breaks; to restore him to his preaccident state through modern medical technology. EMS personnel at the accident site did collect smashed body

parts and did rush them to King's Hospital, where doctors attempted microsurgical reattachment of such parts to restore Mr. Dumpty to normal health.

(8) Rather than restoring Plaintiff "good as new," malpractice by consulting physicians and operating physicians instead turned Mr. Dumpty into "bad as old," by failing to put him back together again in a manner consistent with accepted medical technique.

(9) Statements given by attending physicians in Document A331-C indicated "Patient arrived at hospital in a vegetative state." This report led to callous treatment endured by the Plaintiff and has caused him to undergo numerous cosmetic surgeries in an effort to restore his well-being.

(10) Prior to surgery Mr. Dumpty had an oval-shaped frame, consistently smooth in all areas, with no obvious cracks, crevices, fissures, overlays, holes, rough edges, bumps, bruises, or other disfigurements. Rather than painstakingly reassembling Plaintiff, surgeons callously and with obvious disregard for the Plaintiff's well-being did not attempt to refit recovered pieces, instead putting them anywhere deemed appropriate; therefore body parts were reattached in the wrong places. As a result, Mr. Dumpty's once smooth complexion became rough and coarse; Plaintiff's once oval-

shaped frame lost all recognizable shape, body parts overlapped, and other significant body parts were cracked and broken as surgeons forced them into place with disregard for Plaintiff's well-being. Rather than employing the services of a certified plastic surgeon or glueist, responsibility for restoring Mr. Dumpty to his former state was left in the hands of unqualified physicians.

(11) Such physicians did fail to maintain the operating theater in antiseptic condition. Patient suffered serious postoperative mold complications due, it is contended, to the presence of the King's horses in said operating room. Such horses were present without Board certification and were not licensed by the King to practice medicine.

(12) The King's horses and the King's physicians failed to restore Plaintiff to his former state, due to negligence, carelessness, and a complete lack of refrigeration, and are therefore liable for damages under the statutes of this kingdom.

PETITIONERS: Jack, George, Peter, Maria, Mary, Ronald, Steven, Dennis, Eileen, Tony, Jane, Kumbasha, Emily, Pearl, Carl, Benjamin, Caroline, Andrew, Kee-Wa, Jonas, Diana, William, Mary Margaret, Victor, Harry, Samuel, Juan, Georgia, Jake, Martin, Thomas, Regina, Jeffrey, Oliver, Tammy, Irwin, Paul, Leonard, Isiah, Richard Milhouse, Warren, Mark, Judy, Jessica, Molly, Lindsay, Ulysses, Xavier, Junior, Theodore, Kenneth, et al.

V.

ESTATE OF OLD LADY WHO LIVED IN A SHOE

Notice of Summary Judgment

FOR THE COURT: Judge Solomon

have before me an application from the petitioners, Jack, George, et al., to declare null and void the finding of the First Court that the executor of the estate of the deceased, Old Lady, acted in good faith and correctly in awarding all of her earthly possessions to her oldest son, Marty.

THE FACTS: The deceased, the Old Lady, age undetermined, died intestate, without providing a last will and testament outlining her wishes for the disposal of her estate, be it ever so humble.

THE PROPERTY: Under provisions of the law, the Office of the Sheriff did conduct an extensive search for all known possessions of the deceased and did provide the Court with an inventory. Such possessions included

(1) an old shoe, size very large;
(2) miscellaneous furnishings for (1) (above).

THE PETITIONERS ask that the Court find that the Old Lady was noncompos mentis at the time of her death, meaning she was incapable of understanding the consequences of her actions and did not intend to disinherit all of her children by the lack of a will. Petitioners state, "The Old Lady who lived in a shoe had so many children she didn't know what to do about providing for them all." So rather than divide her possessions, she believed that the lack of a will would result in all her survivors continuing to live in their shoe in harmony. There is no evidence that she desired her eldest child to inherit her estate to the exclusion of all other children.

DECISION: The law speaks quite clearly and often eloquently on matters such as this. In instances in which an individual dies without providing for his or her heirs in a specific manner, such property is subject to the law of primogeniture. Under this law, the firstborn or eldest son shall be entitled to inherit the entire estate. "The superior or exclusive right to succeed to the estate of the ancestor is possessed by the eldest son by right of seniority of birth and to the exclusion of younger sons." There is no mention in any way or manner of the rights possessed by female children; in fact, the law of *noget squat* specifically excludes female children in the presence of a male sibling from receiving any legal inheritance in this situation.

Therefore, it is the decision of the Court that the eldest son, Marty, shall be entitled to receive sole possession of the shoe and all it contents.

Judgment of the Lower Court affirmed.

OAK V. GEPETTO

Opinion of Judge Wood
U.S. District Court
Special Branch

HE FACTS: The Plaintiff, Oak, has come before this Court to plead for the return of his natural-born offspring, a minor hereinafter referred to in this proceeding as "Pinocchio." The Plaintiff claims that this minor was violently abducted approximately eight years ago by the

Defendant, Gepetto. Plaintiff further claims that said Gepetto has brainwashed the minor Pinocchio until he no longer has the ability to determine truth from lie, fact from fiction. Plaintiff demands immediate return of the minor in addition to an order from this Court prohibiting said Gepetto from having any further contact in any form with said minor Pinocchio.

The Defendant, Gepetto, counterclaims that said minor Pinocchio was barely surviving when he found him; that he was living in the woods in rotting conditions; that he was completely without clothes, without adult supervision of any kind; that he was growing up misshapen and twisted. Respondent claims to have saved the life of said minor Pinocchio and raised him as he would have his own child, to respect the truth and with good manners.

At trial the Plaintiff, Oak, testified as follows: I was living peacefully in the Black Forest with a growing family when suddenly, and without warning or provocation, I was brutally attacked by a then unknown individual with a deadly weapon. This then unknown assailant proceeded to rip and saw me asunder limb from limb, inflicting extreme pain and anguish. I was totally and completely defenseless. I could not leave. This attack left me, literally, as stiff as a board. When I recovered from the shock induced by this assault, I discovered that my beloved offspring, to whom I had given life and limb, had been abducted.

Under the circumstances there was nothing I could do. My roots were deep in the community, and it simply was not possible for me to pack my trunk and search for him. I wanted to go after the person who had taken my limb, but I was stumped. Time passed, and while I recovered from my physical wounds, emotionally I never got over this loss. I wept for my child. I knew he had been completely cut off from his own kindling. Eventually a little birdie told me that my offspring was living in the village with a so-called woodcarver named Gepetto. I learned that Gepetto had turned my offspring into his puppet, forcing him to fulfill his desires. Moreover, Pinocchio, as I learned he was called, had attempted to flee his captor and during that time was in grave jeopardy.

While ensconced in the Gepetto domicile, young Pinocchio was deprived of any knowledge of his heritage. When Pinocchio began sprouting, a natural process, and growing his own limb, Gepetto convinced him that this was, in fact, a deformity caused by failure to adhere to Gepetto's beliefs, thereby further brainwashing the poor sapling. There can be no question that Pinocchio suffered and continues to suffer from a warped sense of reality and that he would be much better served by being returned to his own bed.

The Defendant, Gepetto, testified at trial that: [i]n order to appreciate the depth and impact of my relationship with the subject of this proceeding, it is necessary to understand how this relationship began. When I first came upon him, Pinocchio was unrecognizable as the individual he is today. He was not wearing any clothes, he was totally exposed to the elements, unable to respond to any stimulus. He was completely devoid of emotion and did not speak. When I asked him what he was doing in the forest, he did not respond. When I carried him home in my arms, he did not object.

From that first moment it was clear to me that he was rotting away inside. My only desire was to save him. I took him with me to my small shop and day after day tried to shape him into the kind of young boy I could be proud of. I fed him and clothed him. As he had never been exposed to civilization, I tried to teach him by example; when necessary, I was a stern disciplinarian. But there were never any strings attached. He was free to stay with me as long as he wanted to. I had carved out our own little world.

While Pinocchio never did become a chip off the old block, he learned many lessons. It is true that for much of his childhood he was completely dependent upon me. But one day my fondest wish came true. It was as if a miracle had happened: Pinocchio became independent. And, to be honest, he quickly got bored with the life we led together. The things we had once enjoyed no longer seemed to be of interest to him. He barely spoke to me. At times he did not tell the truth. He would make up unbelievable stories, expecting me to believe him. Once, for example, when I threatened to punish him for being out all night, he claimed that a witch had turned him into a donkey. Nothing that I did was good enough for him. He accused me of being completely out of touch with reality. In short, Pinocchio had become a teenager.

I began to suspect that there was something physically wrong with him when he developed a rare dermatological problem that caused excess swelling to his nose and subjected him to ridicule from his friends. He told me he believed his nose grew when he told a lie, but I suspected he was lying about that. The truth, I believe, was that the swelling was caused by a deer tick bite.

Finally, one day we argued and he left my home. There was nothing I could do to stop him, as I had no legal hold on him. Weeks later I was able to find him and bring him home with me, where he presently resides.

It is my hope that the Court will understand that for the welfare of this child it is best he be left in my keeping, and that I be awarded custody until the time of his eighteenth birthday.

DR. ROOT, COURT-APPOINTED PSYCHOLOGIST, testified in court as follows: This is an extremely complex and unusually sad situation. On three separate occasions I have interviewed the minor herein described. On each occasion I conducted lengthy interviews. Although said subject is anxious to please and willing to respond, it is obvious he has deep-seeded psychological problems. He shows symptoms of severe disassociation, an extreme lack of ego causing him to overcompensate, leading to disillusions of grandeur and a total inability to distinguish reality from fantasy. While outwardly showing initial signs of a manic-depressive disorder, inwardly he may or may not be suffering from the initial stages of schizophrenia.

There is also a suggestion of the presence of mind-altering drug use.

According to the subject, he has no memories of his early childhood. His memory begins at age seven, when he recalls awakening to find an older man hovering above him, holding a large carving knife. The man and the boy lived alone. The man attempted to gain the boy's confidence by bestowing upon him material possessions, but in fact the subject was under his complete domination. This man controlled the purse strings, and the subject was unable to move without his permission.

Undoubtedly because of this extreme control, this manic-possessive behavior, the subject created a rich fantasy life in which he had complete freedom. These fantasies, which he recalls vividly, include one in which he was turned into a donkey. It is important to note that Freud equated the presence of a donkey in a dream with the more common term, ass, which also refers to the posterior portion of the human body. Such sexual references cannot possibly be overlooked in the correct diagnosis of this patient.

Subsequently the subject dreamed that the older man was swallowed by a whale. A whale's mouth is a large, dark opening, which Freud often compared to a tunnel, another obvious sexual metaphor. The subject claims he saved the life of the older man by causing the whale to sneeze, expelling the older man and the subject onto the shore, representing safety. By making himself the lifesaving hero of this dream, the subject is satisfying the needs of a damaged superego.

While the fundamental meaning of such fantasies can easily be explained, it is far more difficult to determine their genesis. Rarely have I interviewed anyone with such deeply repressed memories of their early childhood. A clue to that might be the claim made by the subject that his nose started growing when he told a lie. The belief in growing body parts is a common phenomenon, but it is most often associated with the stomach or feet. The Michigan Board Tests (1983–86) seem to support a conclusion that an individual's claim that his or her nose is growing may suggest the presence of hallucinogenic drugs. A search of the guardian's household uncovered significant amounts of glue, which the guardian claimed was a work-related tool. The effects of glue sniffing on young people is quite well documented: among primary symptoms are the perception that the nose or, in extreme cases, the entire head is becoming enlarged, as well as the creation of vivid fantasies often involving so-called fairy godpeople. So while it cannot physically be proved that the subject did participate in glue-sniffing activities, certainly there is every reason to suspect that this is the source of his erratic behavior.

Under any circumstances this is not a healthy environment for a growing child. The lack of any female presence and the easy availability of mind-altering substances are both clear danger signals. It is my belief that the child should be removed from this environment as soon as possible.

However, returning him to his natural parent after all these years is not a suitable alternative. The forest is no place for a boy lacking the most elemental survival skills. While an ongoing relationship with this branch of his family would be beneficial, putting down roots in the forest would deprive the subject of all the positive benefits of civilization.

CONCLUSION: Nothing could be more difficult for a judge than awarding custody of a child to one parent while depriving other parents of those rights. Yet such decisions must be made. In these cases there is little precedent upon which a judge might rely, as every case is the first and only case of its particular nature. Do we award custody of the child to the natural parent who gave it life or the adoptive parent who gave it love? Or do we simply hire a rail splitter and chop the child in half?

This case is complicated by the existing psychological problems of this child. It is clear that while the woodcarver Gepetto loves the child, he is simply incapable of creating the healthy environment necessary for a successful upbringing. Conversely, while the rights of the natural parent are clear, moss is simply not a nutrient for a growing child.

Additionally, the probability that this child has used and may continue to use drugs renders all claims moot. The drug problem must be resolved before any final determination can be made. Therefore, I hereby remand this child to the custody of the Betty Ford Clinic for a complete drug analysis and an initial detoxification program. When he has recovered sufficiently to fully comprehend the matters at issue here, as well as distinguish the difference between reality and fantasy, we will revisit this case.

Kingdom v. Prince Charming

Summation of Mr. Clarion
(Prosecution for Kingdom)

ood afternoon, ladies and gentlemen of the jury. You have before you what I believe to be a simple but vitally important task. It is your job—nay, your privilege—to be in a position to protect the virtue of every woman in this kingdom. For these past few weeks you have sat here listening to the disgraceful tale of how one man, a pillar of this kingdom, knowingly and persistently took advantage of the fair damsels of this community. You have heard witnesses describe how he made promises to them, how he gave them hope for a better life and then, after he had had his way with them, betrayed them. You have heard witness after witness describe how he gained their confidence, then dismissed them forever after. And you have seen the evidence, the so-called glass slipper. The slipper that could not possibly have ever been worn.

Ladies and gentlemen, in a few minutes you will retire to the jury room and determine the fate and reputation not only of the accused, but of the entire kingdom. It is an awesome burden. But let that verdict be a clear message to all who come here: Our damsels are not for trifling. This is a place of chivalry. So I beseech you, ladies and gentlemen, beseech you, to reach the only possible verdict in this case: You must find that this prince is not so charming! And that he is guilty as charged of sexual abuse!

Let us take a few moments to review what you have heard and seen in this courtroom. The basic facts of this sordid case are not in dispute. Let's begin by examining the testimony of the Defendant, the Prince, himself. He admits that this all began the night he attended the annual 1,500-crown-a-plate ball at the Royal Palace. As befitting a prince, he danced with many different women. But then, he claimed, toward the end of the evening a mysterious stranger arrived, a beautiful woman no one in the kingdom had ever seen before. He danced with her for approximately one hour. Close dancing, slow dancing. And yet, according to the Prince's own testimony, he never learned her name. Think of that. They were dancing closer to one another than I am to you, but not once the entire time did he think to ask her what her name was? Does that sound reasonable to you? A charming prince, a beautiful woman, and he failed to ask something as basic as "By the way, what's your name?" How convenient for him, as things turned out. What did they speak about during that time period? The weather in the kingdom? Archery? Perhaps he told her the latest Goth joke. Maybe she shared her favorite witch's brew formula. But he claims he didn't even ask her her name. If you believe that, I've got a little gingerbread house to sell you.

Next, according to the Prince, as the clock began striking midnight, this unidentified woman ran out of the ballroom without even giving the Prince her address. Hard to believe? Well, how about this. The only thing she left behind was a single glass slipper—in fact, this very glass slipper, People's Exhibit 43-1. Finally, according to the Prince, he combed the kingdom far and wide in search of this mystery woman, promising to marry the damsel whose foot fit into that shoe.

Ladies and gentlemen, please. Does this make any sense at all? It is so clearly a subterfuge, an alibi, a fraud, to cover one of the greatest con jobs in the history of this kingdom. What it really is, and what the evidence bespeaks, is that this entire story was created for the Prince to satisfy his abhorrent sexual desire . . . his foot fetish.

I will prove that to you. Let's examine the evidence. First, let us look once again at this highly unusual item, the so-called glass slipper. Think of it, ladies and gentlemen. Of all the different materials in the world from which shoes or boots or slippers might be made, of all the various types of leather and skins and wood and even chain mail, certainly the last material anyone would choose is glass. Yet the defense would have you believe that this mystery woman was wearing glass slippers. You'll notice that glass cannot be bent, it has no flexibility at all. But you are supposed to accept the fact that this mystery woman danced for more than an hour in this glass shoe. How? How could she even move in glass slippers? The answer, of course, is that she couldn't, and that she doesn't even exist.

But let us go further. I haven't even mentioned the inherent danger in wearing glass shoes. One slip in this slipper . . . Well, I'm sure you can visualize the bloody results yourself.

Finally, you heard the expert testimony of the kingdom cobbler Thomas McAn, who said . . . Let me quote him precisely:

QUESTION: Mr. McAn, have you ever in your more than fifty years in the business heard of shoes being made of glass?

ANSWER: I never heard of any such thing. I mean, I think it would be very difficult to do. Soon as you tried to nail on the soles . . . that's it, no more shoe.

And, in fact, the defense has been unable to produce another pair of glass slippers made anywhere at any time, and they failed to do so because it could not be done.

Next, let us more carefully examine the Prince's claim that this mystery woman fled the ball at midnight in an ornate carriage driven by a coachman and pulled by six white horses. I ask you, gentle-folk of the jury, where is this carriage? What happened to it? The Horse-Drawn Vehicle Bureau has absolutely no record of any such carriage being registered in the kingdom. And where are those six white horses? And this coachman? Who is he? Why hasn't he appeared in this courtroom to support this story? Because he doesn't exist, that's why. No, like everything else in this fairy tale, the carriage, the coachman, and the six horses are part of an elaborate ruse by the accused to divert the attention of this Court from the facts of this case.

Finally, let us look at the so-called search organized by the accused. And that, ladies and gentlemen, is why we are here in this room. The search for the nonexistent mystery woman. The search that enabled the Prince to fulfill his hidden sexual desires. The search that allowed him to touch and fondle the feet of so many once innocent women of this kingdom. Let us take just one moment to review some of the damning testimony you heard. I'm sure you remember the handmaiden Diana Freewoman. I'm sure you remember her tears when she told you:

DIANA FREEWOMAN: For a poor maid like me, this was the only real hope I ever had to escape my life of misery. If the shoe fit, I would become a princess. So I joined the long line. I'll never forget the look in the eyes of the Prince as he held my foot in his hands, rubbing it gently, kneading my toes. I could see a strange look in his eyes, as if the Devil himself—

DEFENSE: Objection, Your Honor. There is no accusation of blasphemy here.

THE COURT: Sustained. The witness will refrain from any mention of the presence of the Devil, please.

DIANA FREEWOMAN: I'm sorry. Well, it was a really strange look as he caressed my foot. And then he tried that glass slipper on my foot. It was the biggest shoe I'd ever seen. When it didn't fit, he just smiled at me and said, "Too bad." And then I was dismissed. I was so humiliated.

"And then I was dismissed." This poor, poor girl, falling for the oldest line in the kingdom. A chance to be princess. And there was much more. Remember the testimony of Leticia Goodbody:

LETICIA GOODBODY: He seemed so open and honest, not like most of the men I meet. But when he started rubbing my feet his whole manner changed. He closed his eyes and began breathing heavily. And then, when he made me try on that hideous shoe . . .

Twelve different women recounted similar experiences with this . . . this Prince. Woman after woman, foot abused. Then, finally, at the last minute, what did the defense do? They produced a surprise witness, the mystery woman herself, who claimed the only reason she had come forward was to save the handsome Prince.

Cinderella, she called herself. A woman who works by day as a poor stepsister, who has nothing to her name and so has nothing to lose by claiming to be the mystery woman. Cinderella. She, supposedly, attended the ball that night and caught the Prince's fancy. She, supposedly, was the woman he was searching for when he rubbed and fondled feet from far and near. And you are supposed to believe that. Well, I know you are too smart for that.

And what did this Cinderella have to say for

herself? Well, if you believe her, a fairy godmother appeared and with the flip of a wand dressed her in finery. The missing coach? Well, of course, it was turned back into a pumpkin. A pumpkin, not even a watermelon. The coachmen and horses? Mice, who scattered into fields, where they could conveniently not be called to testify. And finally, the glass slipper itself.

Does the defense believe you people are still living in the Dark Ages? Do they honestly believe you would accept such a tale? I have seen some strange things in my life, I've come to accept the fact that not everything can be explained. A pumpkin transformed into a handsome carriage? Well, I once bought a carriage that turned out to be a lemon. Horses that turned into mice? The truth is I've bet on a few horses that turned out to be dogs. And sadly, even in this kingdom, we all know of men who acted like rats. But there is one thing even this mystery witness, even Cinderella, could not explain. . . .

This Cinderella claimed that the glass slipper came from her foot. Oh, ladies and gentlemen of the jury, Thom McAn showed you how a shoe is measured. He proved to you that this slipper was a size fourteen. Size fourteen! Ladies and gentlemen of the jury, has there ever been a woman in all the world who would admit that she had a size fourteen foot? Would any woman, under threat of being burned at the stake, really admit that?

"Never" is the only answer you can accept to that question. Never. And so you have it. The proof. The smoking shoe. All the evidence you need to convict this . . . this notorious footman. There can be no doubt in your mind. There can be no hesitation when you walk into that room. You must send a clear and unequivocal message that can be heard throughout this kingdom, that even a man of his station, even a prince, cannot take advantage of innocent women in this place. Ladies and gentlemen of the jury, you must find the accused guilty as charged.

The prosecution rests.

Beauty v. Beast

Application to Abrogate, Nullify,
Rescind, Withdraw, Annul, and/or
Otherwise Revoke an Existing
Prenuptial Agreement between
the Petitioner, Beauty, and
the Respondent, Beast

he petitioner warrants that nine years, four months, and two days prior to the date of this filing, the petitioner, Beauty, did willingly but without benefit of legal counsel agree to and sign what in law is commonly referred to as a "prenuptial agreement," a legal document signed prior to marriage in which marrying parties do agree to a disposition of assets should said marriage fail to endure. The petitioner does not contest this fact.

(2) This agreement (Exhibit A) did state that in the event petitioner and respondent did not live happily ever after, the Plaintiff would be entitled to a specific but limited portion of the funds, estate, and all properties owned then or to be acquired during the time of said marriage. This agreement limited such participation in the assets of the Beast to two percent (2%) of his total assets and no more than five percent (5%) of all assets gained during that period during which Beauty and the Beast resided together. It was also stipulated that these funds would be bestowed and distributed entirely at the discretion of the Beast and that Beauty shall/should be entitled to continue living a lifestyle commensurate with that she enjoyed during the period of cohabitation. Petitioner will not contest these facts.

(3) BUT AND/OR HOWEVER, such agreement did not sufficiently or specifically address consequences arising from the desire of the respondent, Beast, to end this marriage, contrary to the wishes and desires of the petitioner, Beauty. This agreement also did not anticipate the four children born to this couple during their marital years.

(4) BUT AND/OR HOWEVER, this agreement did not anticipate the reversal of fortune of said Beast, including the loss of several income-producing properties, resulting in the precipitous decline in the total value of all assets. Said agreement also did not anticipate the extremely high level of inflation resulting in a dramatic increase in the cost of goods and services necessary to the continued well-being of this family. Therefore this combination of factors had reduced the real value of this agreement far below that either anticipated or desired by both parties when such and said agreement was mutually agreed to and signed.

(5) THEREFORE, said agreement does not adequately compensate Beauty and such heirs as exist in a manner that would allow them to maintain the lifestyle to which they have become accustomed and to which the Beast agreed in this document, and therefore, said document should be considered null and void and should be abrogated, rescinded, withdrawn, annulled, and/or otherwise revoked and replaced with a court-ordered disposition of assets owned or controlled by the Beast, and failing that, this document should be replaced with court-ordered support payments to be made on a timely basis of such scale as to enable petitioner to continue to support her family

in a manner approximating that enjoyed during the marital years.

(6) THE FACTS: Petitioner was coerced into signing this agreement. Eight years ago the plaintiff was the simple daughter of a merchant, home educated, an innocent maiden who was forced to share an abode with the respondent to relieve real threats to the family, specifically the father, of the petitioner. Said father, after partaking of the hospitality of the Beast, admittedly did rip, tear, and cause to come asunder a single rose from the property of the Beast. Beast thereupon threatened said father with capital punishment for the "crime" of rose robbing. Beast provided an alternate sentence to the father: If his daughter, the petitioner, would reside within the confines of the Beast's estate for one year, the sentence passed upon the father would be revoked. After discussing this with his family the father agreed to these terms.

(7) At great personal sacrifice, giving up all she knew and to whom she was known, the petitioner did leave her abode and reside in common with the Beast. All parties to this binding contract agreed that the term "reside with" would be specifically limited to a physical presence on such premises as designated by the Beast and would not include any physical contact whatsoever. All parties involved

agreed that this contractual provision was properly observed.

(8) STATE OF MIND: At the time the petitioner agreed to cohabit with the Beast, his state might properly be described as "the unfortunate victim of a wicked fairy." In all physical traits he more closely resembled an individual identified as a member of the animal kingdom than those traditionally known as human beings. Rather than a nose he had a long snout. His ears were long and extended beyond the rim of his head. His entire body was covered by hair. He had a tail. Instead of the common hands and fingers, he had paws and claws. Such physical handicaps did cause the Beast to create a solitary existence. He lived completely alone. He had no known friends. He spent his days doing nonproductive work. Such traits have previously been described by the psychiatric community as being most common among individuals suffering from severe inferiority complexes, often bordering on excessive manic depression.

(9) While he existed in such a state, Beauty did come to fulfill all obligations under the contract agreed to between said Beast and her father. She did share a common residence, and a nonphysical relationship did grow between them. Beauty, void of all knowledge of this curse and believing the

Beast to be, in fact, of his own mind and body, did fulfill completely all contractual terms.

(10) CHANGE OF STATUS: There came a time at which the petitioner requested and was granted temporary relief from contractual terms, allowing her furlough in which to visit her family. She left the residence with permission and goodwill and proceeded to return to her familial residence, at which time and place she enjoyed the familial bonds to which she was otherwise grievously deprived. After several days she did become aware through mitigating circumstances that the Beast was suffering a severe distress reaction occasioned by her absence. A feeling human being, the petitioner experienced great sympathy toward the plight of the afflicted Beast and did return immediately to the aforementioned residence.

(11) PETITIONER SAVES LIFE OF RESPONDENT: On arrival at said premises, petitioner found respondent to be extremely weak, apparently stricken with an illness of a nondetermined, nondiagnosed, and arguably psychosomatic nature. Respondent complained of difficulty in breathing and severe heart pains. Overcome by sympathy for said respondent, petitioner did willingly, of her own accord, without prompting, lean over and kiss respondent.

(12) CHANGE OF STATUS OF RESPON-
DENT: This kiss-of-life caused to occur an immediate and dramatic transformation, during which
the respondent was physically altered from an individual resembling a beast in all physical character-
istics to a handsome prince. Respondent claimed
that prior physical appearance resulted from an
altercation with a wicked fairy. Respondent admit-
ted that the kiss administered by petitioner of her
own free will was the only antidote for such penal-
ty. At that same time, respondent did suggest, ask,
request, and otherwise beseech petitioner to abandon her blood relatives and exist in a marital state
with him. And at such time respondent did suggest,
ask, request, and otherwise beseech petitioner to
agree to a prenuptial pact outlining distribution of
his assets in the event said nuptials should not pre-
vail for a substantial period of time. The petitioner, having just witnessed this transformation, can
psychologically be described as "being in a state of
confusion occasioned by such change as never
before experienced" and therefore completely
unable to make real and rational decisions based on
the actual events having occurred. So without
counsel to which she was entitled and, as a matter
of law, obligated to consult, the petitioner did
agree to such terms as outlined by the Prince.

These terms eventually proved heinous in all aspects to the continued health and well-being of the petitioner and such heirs as now exist. In legal terms, the petitioner might be termed to be *Princess Simplea.*

(13) FAILURE TO LIVE HAPPILY EVER AFTER: Unfortunately this cautionary tale precludes any claim whatsoever by either party that the resulting nuptials concluded in an ending properly defined as "happily." It is the position of the petitioner that in addition to the solely cosmetic change experienced by the respondent, there occurred concurrently a more substantive change, i.e. a complete reversal of personality. At the outset of this relationship the respondent might accurately be described as "a beast on the exterior, a prince on the interior." However, once transformed, due entirely to the actions, dedication, and selflessness of the petitioner, the respondent thereupon became "a prince on the outside, a beast on the inside." It is charged in divorce papers filed by the petitioner that the respondent, while fulfilling his spousal obligations, did also engage in extramarital activities in extremis. The petitioner can provide substantial evidence that the respondent did engage in carnal activities with eight or more village maidens while the petitioner was entirely

engaged in providing a happy castle for him and producing his family. These extramarital activities did cause substantial pain and suffering, ridicule, emotional distress, and physical danger from prolonged contact with a variety of maidens. The petitioner and respondent did engage in at least several loud and lengthy discussions about these activities, and during one such encounter the respondent did knowingly accuse the petitioner of "gaining weight," an unusually cruel and harmful attack on the emotional state of the petitioner. These prolonged discussions did occur more frequently until it became no longer viable for the petitioner to cohabit in the castle of the respondent.

(14) PRECEDENT: Various aspects of this petition have been litigated previously, and there exists substantial precedent to support the claims made by the petitioner. In *Queen v. Rumpelstiltskin* the Court held that an individual, in that case Queen, could not be compelled to fulfill a contract, however valid such contract, if provisions of said contract forced either party into performing actions that otherwise would not be considered legal. In that case the issue was involuntary servitude to fulfill an obligation entered into by Queen. The Court said, "No party to a contract can legally waive such rights as to put them in such a posi-

tion as they are compelled by said contract to perform activities or services deemed illegal under the existing statutes of that municipality, as such rights are beyond the scope of the individual to waive. Specifically, *'Such contracts negotiated, agreed to, or signed in a situation in which any contracting party may be responding to pressure, duress, or other external factors, causing them to act against their own self-interest, are hereby held to be invalid and cannot be used to compel any action.'"* Having previously witnessed the respondent transformed from Beast to Prince can be seen by the Court to have created a situation rife with pressure and duress, which therefore would invalidate any agreements made in that state of mind.

(14i) In *Kingdom* v. *Old Lady Who Lives in a Shoe* (cit. 34 part b, ex parte 145), in which the Defendant (Old Lady) attempted to provide for many children by contracting for their services prior to their taking residence in the shoe, in direct contravention to an order from the Child Welfare Board, the Court held, "It is imperative that the Court recognize there exists no rights of any individual to proffer, contract for, or in any other way whatsoever accept or agree to any contract concerning the welfare of minor children without the express consent of coherent adult supervisors." It is the contention of the petitioner that by agreeing to and signing this contract while in a state of extreme duress, and without counsel, the rights of the children were compromised and therefore the entire agreement is invalid, as the children were improperly represented in this agreement.

(15) REMEDY: It is within the power of this Court first, to declare said prenuptial agreement to have been signed under duress, at a time in which the petitioner was not in complete possession of faculties, and is therefore invalid; and, second, to replace this agreement with a court-ordered schedule of payments, compelling the respondent to fulfill his paternal obligations to the best of his ability.

Respectfully filed:

O. King Cole

[O. King Cole]

LITTLE RED RIDING HOOD
V.
REGAL PICTURES, INC.

PLAINTIFF alleges Invasion of Privacy,
Trademark Infringement, Violation of
Right of Publicity, and Defamation
of Character

HEREAS and wherefore Little Red Riding Hood, Plaintiff, is a living person, a citizen of this kingdom, with all the rights thereupon granted to her, it is hereby alleged that Regal Pictures, Inc., a division of General Entertainment Ltd., a wholly owned and operated subsidiary of Datsui International, did invade the privacy of the Plaintiff, infringe exclusive trademark rights, and violate a legal right of publicity of the Plaintiff by producing, releasing, and distributing into general release an animated motion picture entitled *The Adventures of Little Red Riding Hood*. This story, held to be a true telling of events occurring in the life of Plaintiff, did hold Plaintiff up to shame and ridicule, causing her extreme emotional pain and anguish. This did also cause Plaintiff irreparable financial harm by rendering her unemployable, and therefore Plaintiff asks for damages of not less than one million dollars ($1,000,000), in addition to 3.5 percent interest in gross receipts of this motion picture, with such gross receipts to be determined under a formula currently approved by Screen Actors Guild.

Little Red Riding Hood is a known figure. She has diligently created a public image by wearing, on any and all occasions, a red riding cape with a red hood. It is in all forms her costume, and it is uniquely associated with her by name. This costume holds a kingdom trademark and is entitled to all the protections given under the trademark laws. Little Red Riding Hood has licensed and continues to hold the exclusive license to this costume under said trademark for instances such as masked balls,

Halloween costumes, school plays, and such events. This is a valuable property, and the licensor has fervently protected this trademark. A negotiated fee is required for each use of this license. Little Red Riding Hood has diligently protected this trademark, and the Court has upheld her ownership in toto of such license.

"Little Red Riding Hood" is a registered trademark. It is wholly owned by the Plaintiff under the name Little Red Riding Hood, Inc., a fiefdom corporation, a subsidiary of Little Red Riding Hood Enterprises. The right to use the name "Little Red Riding Hood" for commercial purposes is granted to licensees under contract in all such matters as deemed appropriate and consistent with the wholesome image projected by Little Red Riding Hood. In many instances Little Red Riding Hood, Inc., has refused to grant companies and/or individuals license to use this name, as association with such products or companies is inconsistent with the protected image of the Plaintiff. Among such companies that have applied for license but have not been so granted are manufacturers of feminine hygiene items, children's lingerie, and tobacco companies.

The Plaintiff, Little Red Riding Hood, has actively defended all attempts to exploit her name and likeness for commercial purposes except those specifically licensed by Plaintiff. She has spent many years creating an image and protecting it from exploitation for commercial gain by anyone without proper commercial license. The motion picture produced, released, and distributed by Regal Pictures, Inc., does defame Plaintiff and can cause real and serious financial harm to any and all enterprises currently in existence or contemplated at any time in the future forever and ever.

Regal Pictures, Inc., did cause to be produced, released, and distributed the animated motion picture *The Adventures of Little Red Riding Hood*, featuring an animated character who wore a red riding cape and a red riding hood consistent in all ways with the trademark-protected costume generally associated with Little Red Riding Hood; moreover, this animated character identified herself as, and answered to the name, "Little Red Riding Hood," a name protected by copyright. In this animated motion picture the character identified as Little Red Riding Hood did leave her home with the intention of taking to her ailing grandmother a basket of goodies, then residing on the distant side of a forest. According to this animated motion picture, the character identified by likeness and name as Little Red Riding Hood did meet a vicious wolf during such trip and did engage in a conversation with this wolf. As depicted in this motion picture, Little Red Riding Hood did inform the wolf that she was on her way to visit her ailing grandmother, thereby communicating to the wolf information that might be considered extremely dangerous to the grandmother. This did cause the wolf to proceed immediately to the grandmother's address, at which time the grandmother was eaten by the wolf. Upon arrival on the premises of Little Red Riding Hood, the wolf did don the garments of the eaten grandmother and proceeded to trick, fool, and charm Little Red Riding Hood into believing the wolf was indeed the ailing grandmother. According to this animated motion picture, Little Red Riding Hood failed to notice that this was a wolf in grandmother's clothing and instead commented only on the big eyes, big ears, and big teeth of this grandmother impersonator. The wolf leaped upon Little Red Riding Hood, inflicting serious injury, and Little Red Riding Hood was saved by hunters who happened to be nearby. This animated story is constructed from whole cloth, bears no resemblance to the truth, and misappropriates the name and likeness of Little Red Riding

Hood for profit in violation of her rights of publicity.

This scenario gives the appearance that Little Red Riding Hood had complicity in the untimely death of her grandmother due to ingestion by the wolf, that Little Red Riding Hood did knowingly hold civil conversations with a wolf, that Little Red Riding Hood failed to recognize a wolf dressed in a bonnet and dressing gown and required the timely assistance of hunters to save her life. This scenario presents Plaintiff as weak, needy, nearsighted, hard of hearing, dependent, and foolish and is not in keeping with the true facts as they are known.

The scenario featured in the animated motion picture *The Adventures of Little Red Riding Hood* is provably false and inconsistent with the true facts as they are known. Little Red Riding Hood did endeavor to take to her ailing grandmother a shopping bag of pharmaceutical drugs intended to assist her recovery, an act of mercy intended to restore the ailing grandmother to good and proper health. She did dress in her trademarked red riding cape and hood. But she did drive to her grandmother's house, using Royal Route 4, making any and all contact with a wolf impossible. She did not meet this wolf. She did not converse with this wolf.

She did not inform this wolf, or any member of the animal family of any kind, that her grandmother was infirm. Upon arriving at the grandmother's house, she did note immediately that all lights had been turned off and all the shades were closed, making it impossible to see more than a few feet. When she endeavored to turn on lights, she was informed, by the wolf impersonating a grandmother, that the light affected her eyes and therefore she did not want any light emitted to the house. This complete lack of light prevented Little Red Riding Hood from seeing the individual lying in her grandmother's bed. Little Red Riding Hood, upon arriving at her grandmother's house, did immediately notice that the voice coming from the bed did not resemble her grandmother's; upon remarking about that, she was informed that the illness had detrimentally affected the vocal cords, thereby causing the known voice of the ailing grandmother to change and making it impossible for Little Red Riding Hood to determine an impostor was on the premises. Little Red Riding Hood, upon arriving at her grandmother's house, did immediately attempt to kiss her grandmother but was warned to maintain a safe distance of approximately fifteen (15) feet from the bed to prevent communication of virus-caused disease, making it impossible for Little Red Riding Hood to determine an impostor was in her grandmother's bed. It is provably false and detrimental to the image created by Little Red Riding Hood to claim that she mistook a wolf for her grandmother. Such a thing did not happen, could not happen, and the portrayal of such an episode has caused and will continue to cause mental distress and serious financial harm to the Plaintiff.

The scenario featured in the animated motion picture *The Adventures of Little Red Riding Hood* did also claim that Little Red Riding Hood was rendered helpless by the wolf in grandmother's clothing and was completely dependent for her life and limb upon the intercession of hunters. This is provably false. As was noted in police reports, the wolf did attack Little Red Riding Hood but was summarily punched, kicked, gouged, and beaten into submission by Plaintiff, who employed her recognized skills in martial arts discipline. This scenario is provably false and will severely impact on the ability of the Plaintiff to portray heroic figures in future endeavors.

Therefore, Plaintiff demands Regal Pictures makes full and complete restitution to Plaintiff for damages suffered and future damages caused by the production, release, and distribution of this animated motion picture, in an amount to be determined by the Court, plus punitive damages, and that Defendants cease and desist from the continued violation of Plaintiff's rights.

Frog Prince
V.
Wicked Witch

A Request for Immediate Injunctive Relief

HEREAS and wherefore the Prince, hereinafter referred to as the Plaintiff, who unjustly and without cause, reason, legal standing, or permission has been accursed by the Wicked Witch, hereinafter referred to as Defendant, and under terms of such curse has been turned for an indefinite period into a frog, and therefore suffered and continues to suffer irreparable damage to his name and reputation, said Frog Prince does hereby request and demand immediate injunctive relief to compel Defendant to lift, remove, take off, undo, and otherwise reverse such curse until such time as a final determination as to the rights of the Plaintiff can be determined by a duly constituted court of law.

FACTS AT ISSUE

ON OR about the sixth day of the third month of this year, the Wicked Witch of the East did knowingly and without any legal basis whatsoever, without cause, and without notice unilaterally invoke and cast such spells, curses, incantations, black magic, and any and all other mystic powers to cause the Plaintiff to be transformed in body from a prince to a frog. Such curse was to be sustained for an indefinite period of time, to be lifted only upon such instance as an official and legally registered princess did knowingly and of her own free will kiss such frog with affection. The application of this curse is a clear violation of the Plaintiff's rights to a free and happy life as guaranteed by the constitution of this kingdom; the application of such curse in perpetuity is a clear violation of the Plaintiff's right to a fair sentence to be administered only after a judgment in a court of law as guaranteed by the constitution of this kingdom; and the application of this curse without the express written permission of a legally constituted body is a clear violation of the Plaintiff's rights as guaranteed by the constitution of this kingdom.

PRIOR TO the illegal application of the invocation, the Plaintiff did enjoy a complete and full life, unhindered by any natural or unnatural limitations. He was able to and did partake completely in all forms of professional work and social entertainment, including but not limited to alcoholic beverages, consorts with females, and amusement by minstrel. While unmarried, he did receive and partake in numerous invitations proper to and befitting a future king. He did ably conduct princely business and by all appearances functioned in a normal, unencumbered manner. He did enjoy the complete respect of citizens of the kingdom and was held in high esteem.

THE IMPOSITION of this curse did significantly and substantially change and alter each and all aspects of the Plaintiff's life. Immediately after the illegal transformation from prince to frog, Plaintiff did cease to receive invitations to events of any kind, and those invitations previously tendered were withdrawn. He was unable to function at all in a princely fashion. Following the imposition of this curse, he was considered to be socially unacceptable and lost favor with the citizens of this kingdom; he became the subject of scorn and ridicule and the object of antiamphibious attacks. This complete failure of all aspects of his social life did engender feelings of inferiority, despair, depression, anger, hostility, embarrassment, and distress.

PRIOR TO the imposition of such curse, the Plaintiff did enjoy a positive reputation in all fields and forms of business activity. His advice and consent for a variety of projects were prized and sought. He participated in many construction, agricultural, and entrepreneurial activities; his good name lent credibility to those business endeavors in which he became involved. Subsequent to the imposition of this curse, any and all business opportunities that existed or might be presumed to exist in the future did cease to exist. The business community shunned the Plaintiff. His advice and consent were neither sought nor appreciated. The

Plaintiff suffered and continues to suffer serious, considerable, and irreparable financial damage due to his inability to actively participate in or oversee financial operations.

PRIOR TO the imposition of such curse, the Prince stood approximately five feet eleven inches tall, weighed 175 pounds, had five toes on each of two feet, five fingers on each of two hands, a ruddy complexion, brown hair, and fine facial features. His physical stature enabled him to participate in all forms of common recreational activity, including but not limited to sitting, walking, running, swimming, mountain climbing, horseback riding, painting and drawing, archery, jousting, dueling, kite flying, bowling, and riding to hounds. Subsequent to the imposition of such curse, Plaintiff was reduced in size to approximately 3½ inches tall, .4 pounds in weight, webbed feet, four fingers, a greenish complexion, no hair, and the characteristic facial features of a frog. His physical stature prevented him from participation in most forms of recreational activity previously enjoyed, although he did excel in jumping and swimming. It is noted that this change in stature resulted in physical danger; i.e., rather than riding to hounds, Plaintiff raced in fear of such hounds.

PRIOR TO the imposition of such curse, Plaintiff spoke proper English, enjoyed singing, laughing, and whistling. Subsequent to the imposition of such curse, Plaintiff has been limited to deep croaking sounds.

PRIOR TO the imposition of such curse, Plaintiff was able to make merry with many and varied damsels of the kingdom and surrounding lands. Subsequent to the imposition of such curse, to satisfy any and all carnal longing, Plaintiff was limited to frogs.

PRIOR TO the imposition of such curse, Plaintiff enjoyed a full and hearty palate of traditional fare, including but not limited to turkey, chicken, beef, hog, lamb, grouse, and fish of various nature. Subsequent to the imposition of such curse, Plaintiff's diet has been limited to flies and bugs.

IN ANY and all forms of normal life, Plaintiff can no longer enjoy and savor those things to which he is entitled under royal birthright and the constitution of the kingdom. It is therefore requested that Defendant be enjoined from continuing the application of such curse and that the Court order such curse be immediately lifted until such time as the proper legally constituted body can render a decision.

THE REMEDY

AS THERE have been no claims made thus far pertaining to or specifically delineating that nature of the injustice upon which the unilateral application of such curse is based, there fails to be any legal issue to be remedied through action in a court of law. However, Plaintiff urges the Court to issue this injunction without prejudice, thus allowing Defendant to reinstate any and all claims to be argued in the proper forum for such disagreement. Therefore, the Defendant, the Wicked Witch, will not suffer any duress, harm, or consequence, nor will standing be lost, by the issuance of an injunction by this Court compelling the Defendant to lift the offending curse until such time as a duly constituted body permits it to be reinstated.

FAILING THAT, Plaintiff has a significantly limited opportunity to fulfill the rules and regulations of such curse, i.e., "if Plaintiff is kissed by a legally recognized princess of her own free will." It is well known by this Court that few regal ladies, of their own volition and desire, will willingly kiss or otherwise feel, fondle, touch, buss, or rub a frog.

PENALTIES AND DAMAGES

PLAINTIFF HAS been and continues to be damaged mentally, physically, and financially by the continued imposition of such curse as herein described in an amount to be determined. Plaintiff reserves the right to take action against the Defendant for any and all monetary damages as may be determined by a court of competent jurisdiction in the future. Nothing in this document or any judgment made by this Court shall be deemed to alleviate Defendant of responsibility for harm and hardship created by the illegal imposition of such curse and the continued hardships created by the illegal imposition of such curse.

THEREFORE, IT is requested by the Plaintiff, the Frog Prince, that the Court immediately order the Defendant to cease and desist imposition of such curse.

Kingdom
v.
Goldilocks

I hereby certify that this is the true record of the remarks made to the jury in summation by Richard Grimm, Esq., speaking for the defense.

Dick Grimm

ood afternoon, ladies and gentlemen of the jury. First, let me thank you for your patience over these long months. I'm not going to take as much of your time as did the esteemed prosecutor because the burden on me is considerably less. I don't have to prove anything. I simply have to bring your attention to the fact that there is reasonable doubt that my client, Goldilocks, broke into the house of the Bear family, sat in their chairs, ate their porridge, damaged their possessions, and slept in their beds, as alleged. It shouldn't take me very long to do that, for in this case there exists far, far more than reasonable doubt; there simply can be no question that the prosecution has failed to prove its case. The prosecution claims they have presented "a pile of hard evidence." A pile of evidence? What do they really offer you? A few slender strands of hairs and fibers. Some DNA. A fingerprint. An eyewitness identification. A purported confession. Traces of porridge found on a pair of stockings. And that is it. That's all. Yet based on that they expect you to convict my client. I think they might better expect some witch to turn the judge into a bullfrog.

Let's examine this so-called evidence. Remember who collected it? Remember who sat on that witness stand and told you a long story about coming to the Bear house late at night? It was Detective Smokey, wasn't it? And right there, right there, is the key to the entire case. Because the prosecution's entire case depends on the credibility of Detective Smokey. Let's look at him again. The fact is that Detective Smokey is . . . like the Bear family, a bear. He is, in fact, a fur man. In the past, as you heard several witnesses testify, Detective Smokey has put his nose to the ground and tracked down and arrested human beings for very minor infractions, while not applying those same strict standards to members of his own Ursidae family. And, I remind you, you heard Detective Smokey himself testify that he found this physical evidence, that he collected it, and that he carried it in for examination himself.

Oh, ladies and gentlemen of the jury. I submit to you that never before in the long and glorious history of this kingdom has the simple phrase "bear witness" been more appropriate. For this detective is a bear, and he is the prime witness against my client. Can you trust him? I ask you, would you leave a fresh fish lying around when Detective Smokey is on the premises?

But let me go further, let me examine this so-called evidence, piece by piece. According to Detective Smokey's testimony, eight long blond hairs consistent with my client, so the prosecution contends, were found on the pillows of Papa Bear, Mama Bear, and Baby Bear. Hair? Okay, we admit it, we confess, you got us. My client has hair! But so does every single female in this jury! Ladies and gentlemen, I'm afraid I must take a moment here to tell you something about which my client is not very proud. My client, the lovely Goldilocks, has not always been so golden. Her real name is Brunetta. Goldilocks is only her . . . her made-up name, her fairy-tale name. Goldilocks's golden locks come from . . . a bottle. As does the blond hair of tens of thousands of women. Yet the prosecutor would like you to believe these hairs could *only* have come from my client. Oh, please, they could have come from anyone with five dollars and the desire to purchase gold in a bottle. These hairs have absolutely no value as evidence.

Now, the DNA. Deoxyribonucleic acid, the so-called genetic fingerprint, the building block of life. According to the prosecution, this DNA stuff was extracted from saliva found on both Papa Bear's and Mama Bear's porridge spoons. Let me refresh your memory. The prosecution expert testified that DNA was, I quote, "the genetic bar code, sort of like the bar codes used on products in the supermarket." Oh, dear. Let me ask you this: How often have you been overcharged at the checkout counter because a clerk scanned the same bottle of ketchup over the electronic reader twice? How many of your purchases did they miss because the bar code was misread? Yet the prosecution asks you to compare my client with a bottle of ketchup. Oh, please.

And let me put this to you: Just where is this magic DNA? Have you seen it? Did they show it to you? No, they did not. They showed you a chart and told you that it was representative of DNA. It was made by DNA. Representative? Representative? If it's so important, let's see it! What is the prosecution trying to hide from you? Ask yourself that. Now, let's look at this chart. It's a lot of dots on what looks like an X-ray. This is DNA? These are the dots that make you unique? Please, ask the prosecutor to show you which dots determine your eye color. Ask him to show you which dots determine whether you are tall or short. They won't be able to. And why? Because this is nothing more than a piece of paper. That's all.

But all right, so we've got these dots on paper. I suspect most of you have played the child's game connect the dots. Believe me, if you could collect all these dots so they spelled out Gold-i-locks, I would have a difficult time standing here in front of you and trying to convince you my client isn't guilty. But that is not the case. Connect the dots on this DNA chart, supposedly the DNA of my client, and what do they spell? Xyrexztdixz, that's what. Not Goldilocks.

Next, let's examine the fingerprints found on Papa Bear's porridge bowl, Mama Bear's porridge bowl, and Baby Bear's porridge bowl. It is absolutely true that never in history have two people been found to have the same fingerprints—but that doesn't mean that no two people have the same fingerprints. It simply means they haven't found them yet, that's all. Think of it this way: Fingerprints are simply ridges and valleys formed by your skin to cover your fingers. With all the people in the world, and all the people who have lived prior to this very day, what are the chances that every single one of them would have the same few lines in different places? Eventually, you are going to run out of different places. It's simply the law of averages. The fact that until today no two people have been found who have the same fingerprints means the odds are getting higher and higher that two people will be found who have exactly the same fingerprints. And who among us would dare say that this is not the case? Admittedly, the few wavy lines found in dry porridge on the side of Papa Bear's bowl are similar in many respects to those of my client. But what does that mean, exactly? It doesn't mean she was in the Bear home; it means she *could* have been in the Bear home. But so were many other people: the Federal Express delivery person; the cable repair man; the mailman. Has anyone thought to take a fingerprint sample from the housekeeper? No, they have not, and the question I am forced to ask is, why? What are they hiding from you? What is it they don't want you to know? We know for certain that the housekeeper touched these bowls. Yet where is her print? There is no way we can know, because Detective Smokey leaped to judgment. This . . . this fur man convicted my client long before there was evidence, then proceeded to build his case around that belief. He was never interested in pursuing anyone else. What we have here is a rush to judgment.

Let us now look at the so-called eyewitness identification. Let us recall the sad, sad testimony of Baby Bear. It was night, the house was dark. Papa Bear announced, "Someone has been sleeping in my bed!" Then Mama Bear announced, "Someone has been sleeping in my bed, too!" Imagine, if you will, Baby Bear's state of mind when he opened the door to his room: scared and confused. And then, in the dim light he saw the rumpled blankets on his bed and knew that someone had been sleeping in his bed, too. Suddenly someone leaped from the bed and ran right at him and then out of the house. Baby Bear, in a panic now, shouted, "And she's still here!"

Ladies and gentlemen of the jury, put yourself in Baby Bear's paws. Alone, in the dark, terrified. Someone leaps at him and runs from the room. What kind of look did he get at this person? How long could he have possibly seen this person? Two seconds? Three seconds? And what kind of look was it? A fleeting glance in a dark room. Was that really long enough to be able to look at my client in the broad daylight of this courtroom and say without pause or hesitation, "That is the person"? I doubt it, I doubt it very much.

It is a long established fact that to members of the Bear community all blondes look alike. I submit to you that Baby Bear indeed saw someone, the same someone who left the blond hairs on his pillow. But did he see my client, Goldilocks? No, he did not.

It doesn't even seem worth my time to discuss this coerced confession with you. You can just throw it out. My client was held by police for almost a full hour without being offered anything to eat or drink. The police are lucky we're not bringing civil rights violation charges against them. By that time she was practically starving. She would have done anything for just a few morsels of food. So when Detective Smokey told her if she signed this confession he would take her to McDonald's . . . I mean, we're in court, let's be honest—if I said I was going to yell at you for a few hours or I was going to take you to McDonald's for thick, juicy hamburgers, those delicious fries, and a crisp, cold soda . . . do you really think you would resist?

No, that confession belongs on the junk heap of fantasy. In just a few moments you will be going into the jury room to consider the evidence. I do not even mention the porridge supposedly found on my client's stockings because . . . who do you think found those stockings? Why, once again, the incredible Detective Smokey. He was all over the place that night, wasn't he? So, when you go into that jury room, I don't want you, my fellow human beings, even to consider the fact that these three bears can sit there all day happily wagging their tails—which you, like my client, do not have—or the fact that they walk on all fours, have hair all over their bodies, don't even speak the same language you do, do not wear clothes, and have been known to devour human beings, people like us. No! I beg you, do not think that this is a vote for compassionate humans against animalistic bears. Don't! Think only of the poor, sloppy case built against my client, the total lack of evidence, and you will have no choice but to find my client not guilty of this serious crime.

I thank you in advance for your verdict.